# A Little Bit BRAVE

ALISON GREEN BOOKS

Logan was a stay-at-home bunny.
His friend Luna was the daring one.
She had new adventures every day.
They sounded quite exciting, but
rather frightening, too.

So whenever Luna said: "Come out with me! It's fun!"

Logan said, "Oh, no.
I'll never go outside. It's far too scary."

At last, Luna had had enough.
"You have to come out with me!"

"No!"
said Logan.

"You're no fun!"
said Luna.

"I'm too scared!"
said Logan.

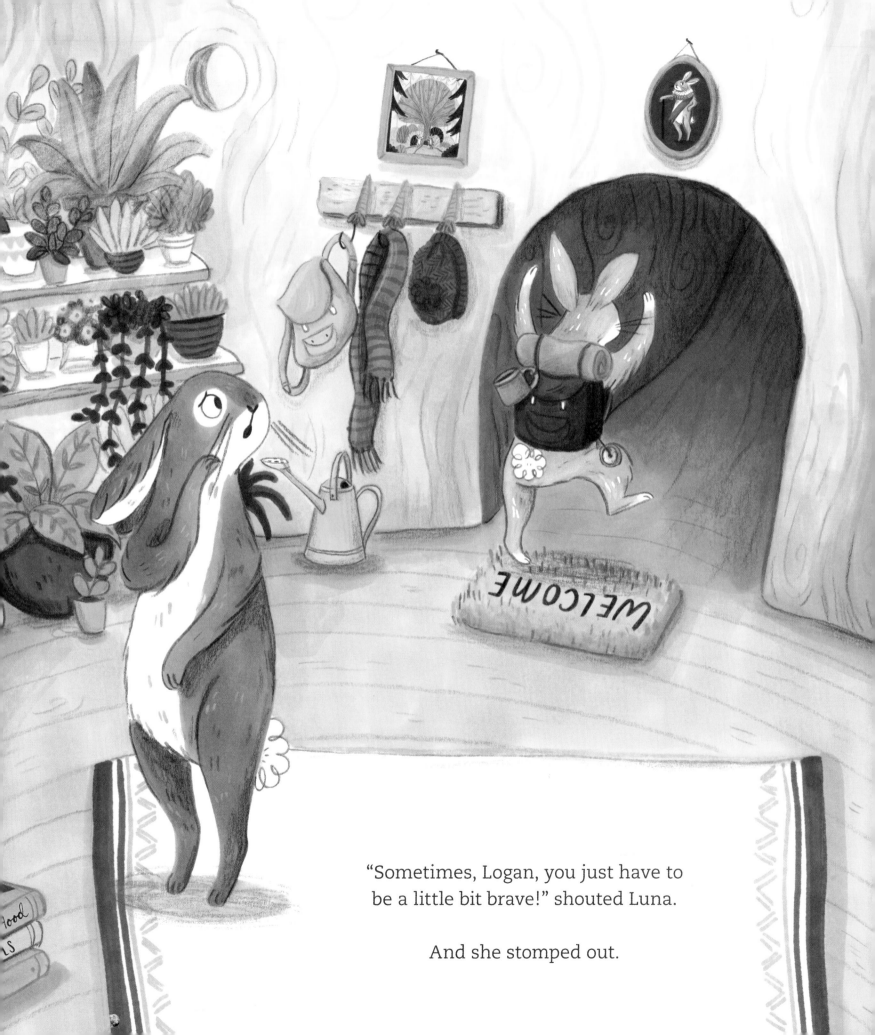

"Sometimes, Logan, you just have to be a little bit brave!" shouted Luna.

And she stomped out.

Logan tried to have
a normal morning.

He watered his
indoor plants.

He dusted his shell collection.

He baked some biscuits. But nothing felt right. He was very upset. Luna had never been angry with him before.

"I have to make it up with her right away," he thought. There was just one problem. Luna was . . .

OUTSIDE!

It would be an adventure, and Logan had
never had one of those. He had no idea
what to pack, so he took a snorkel,
a torch and a tin of biscuits.

biscuits

Then he put on his favourite scarf,
plucked up all his courage, and
tiptoed out . . .

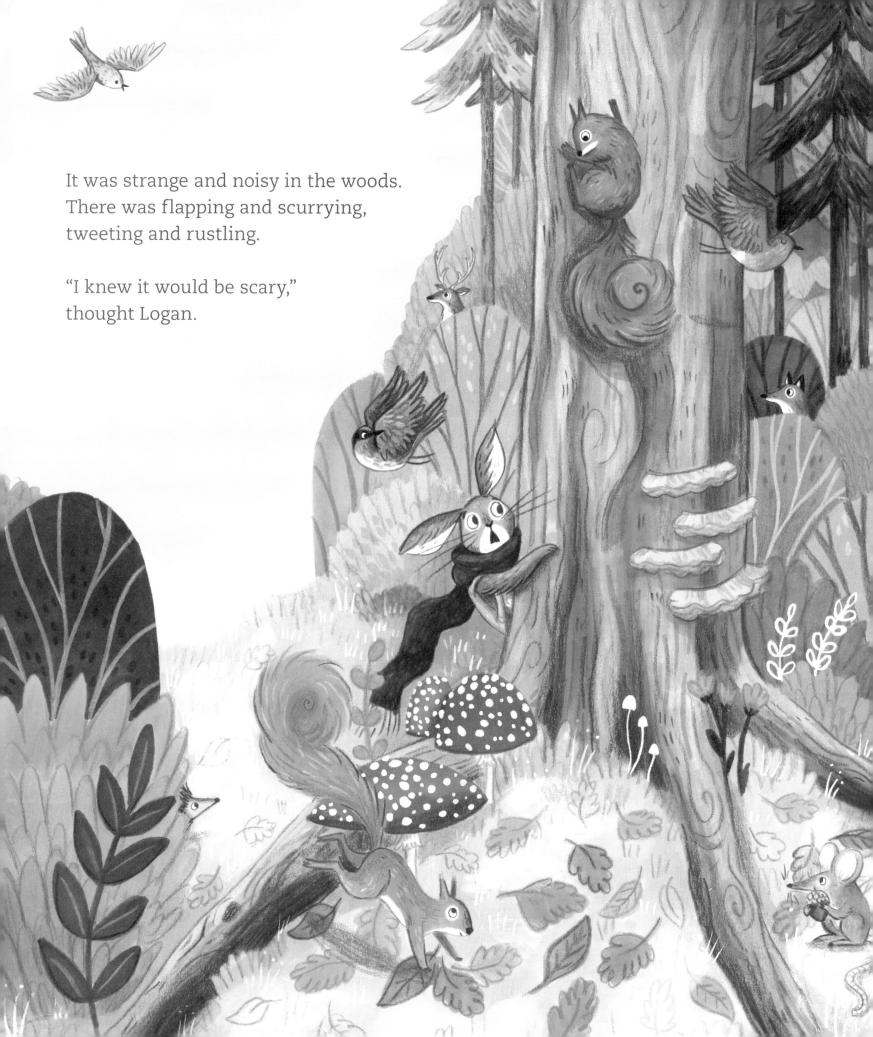

It was strange and noisy in the woods.
There was flapping and scurrying,
tweeting and rustling.

"I knew it would be scary,"
thought Logan.

He took a deep breath
and called:

LUNA!!!

There was no reply . . .

. . . but lots of other animals scampered up. "Luna?" they said. "She's the bravest bunny in the world."

"She dives into the river to collect shells," said an otter.

"She rides round the
forest on my back," said a deer.

"She explores the deep, dark caves
and goes looking for bears,"
said a fox.

"That sounds so scary!"
said Logan.

"But if you do those things, too,"
said a mouse, "perhaps you'll find her."
So that's exactly what Logan did.

First he dived into the river –

# SPLASH!

Brr! It was chilly!
It was lucky he'd
packed his snorkel.

There was a whole new
world underwater. Logan saw
fish and frogs and snails.

But he didn't see Luna.

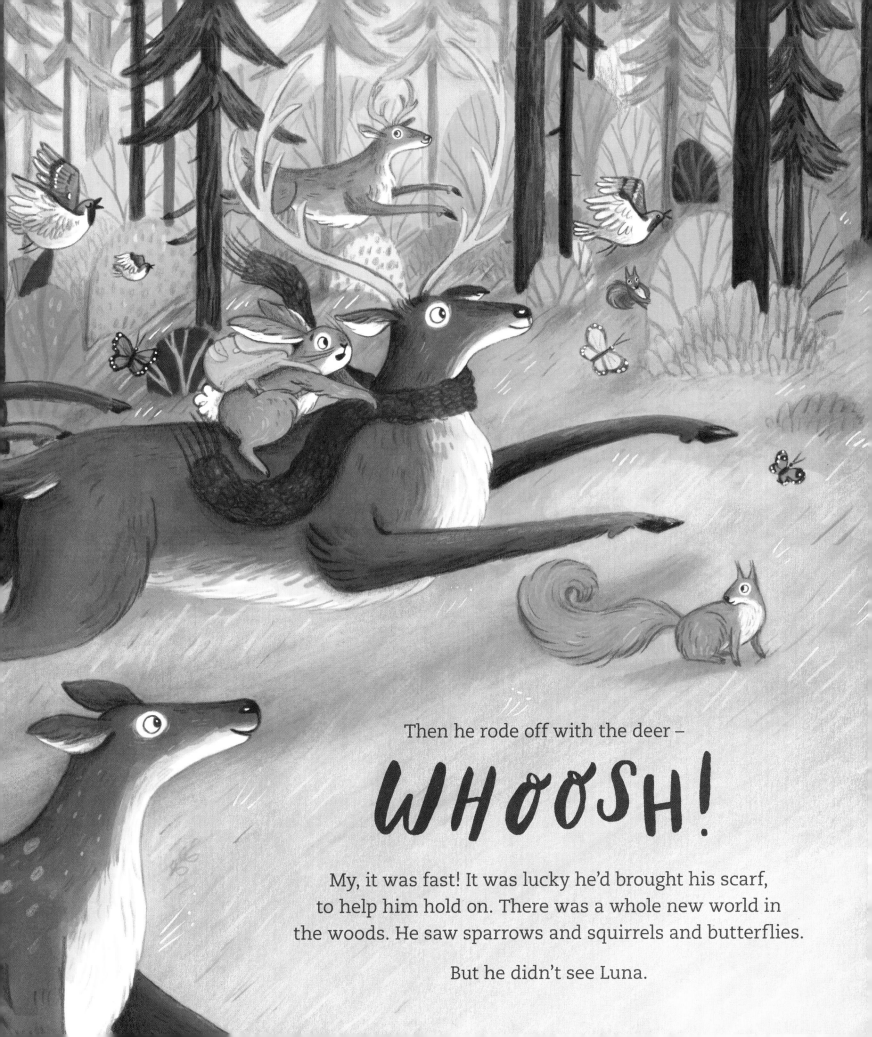

Then he rode off with the deer –

# WHOOSH!

My, it was fast! It was lucky he'd brought his scarf,
to help him hold on. There was a whole new world in
the woods. He saw sparrows and squirrels and butterflies.

But he didn't see Luna.

Then he
tiptoed into
a cave –

# EEK!

It was lucky he'd packed his torch.
There was a whole new world in the dark.
He saw bats and spiders and sleeping bears.
But he didn't see Luna.

Logan was amazed at all the things he'd done.
"If only I could find Luna!" he said.
"She'd be really proud of me."
He was so chuffed, he decided
to have a biscuit.

But before he could open the tin, he heard a shout:

# "STAY BACK, YOU WICKED WOLF!"

That voice sounded very familiar.
In fact, it sounded just like . . .

. . . Luna!
Oh, no! A huge,
hungry wolf was
trying to eat her!

Logan hid behind a tree.
Suddenly he didn't feel brave at all.
"I want to go home!" he whimpered.

But he couldn't let Luna be eaten.
So he picked up his biscuits, plucked
up all his courage . . .

"Eat my biscuits!"

The wolf was
very surprised.

"Biscuits?" he said.
"I don't mind if I do!"
And he gobbled up
the whole lot.

The wolf was very friendly after that.
"That was amazing!" cried Luna.
"When did you become
so brave?"

"I think it started this morning," said Logan,
"when I was baking biscuits."

Luna laughed. "Shall we go home and bake some more?"

"I'd like that," said Logan. "But first . . .

". . . we need another adventure!"

First published in the UK in 2019 by
Alison Green Books
An imprint of Scholastic Children's Books
Euston House, 24 Eversholt Street
London NW1 1DB
A division of Scholastic Ltd
www.scholastic.co.uk
London – New York – Toronto – Sydney – Auckland
Mexico City – New Delhi – Hong Kong
Designed by Zoë Tucker

Text and illustrations copyright © 2019 Nicola Kinnear

HB ISBN: 978 1 407181 78 3
PB ISBN: 978 1 407181 79 0

All rights reserved.
Printed in Malaysia

1 3 5 7 9 10 8 6 4 2

The moral rights of Nicola Kinnear have been asserted.

Papers used by Scholastic Children's Books are made
from wood grown in sustainable forests.